MARRIAGE OF CONVENIENCE

MRS. LOVESTRUCK

This is dedicated to all my dear readers who are in love at first sight
or love at first fight .

Contents

Prologue

This was a dark world where the Almighty lord was the king of all the darkness. His world was divided into five parts and given to his sons Ego, Sin, Mad, Grudge, and Anger. Each brother had his own story to tell .Even when this was a dark world full of evil and wrongs .There was also light and hope .That was bestowed upon them by God himself because he is with evil and good both. lord had arranged matches for his sons .They were angels but each son had to embark on their journey with their angels by themselves. It would be very entertaining for the lord to see how his sons would fight angels and their own evils and all the way falling in love with them.

First Lord wanted to see how his youngest son Anger was doing.

Chapter 1

Lord's fifth state was run by the lord's general because Anger was just four years old. but people did not want a general to run their territory they wanted royal blood to do that .they did not want to follow a general so they killed him and his wife. And began a war. So the lord had to come himself .lord was very angry because he doesn't like his orders to be dismissed so easily it was his appointed general that killed. the lord called his people and addressed them .But they wanted royal blood to run them. They wanted him or his son but not the common general. lord was not happy he wanted to punish them so he made the general's daughter meena the queen of the state and give her his son Anger.

Chapter 2

Lord pov

I knew when meena was born that she was an angel born among the darkness and know that my son would be hers .that was why I made her father a general but my people killed him and his wife .Now there was only one way to punish them. Made a woman, ruler who would rule them. Also who was not of royal blood but every Queen needed a king even if he was only four years old for the fourteen years old meena. This was my world and I was the one who blessed their marriage and no one would go against my word, not ever again. I had faith in anger's queen .she would know how to rule the state .

CHAPTER THREE

Chapter 3

meena pov.

My parents were dead. I was even not there when they needed me. when I was a child of six years lord took me from my home and in the bargain made my father state general. he took me to his palace where he started my education. I was educated in all the subjects. I did not know why but when I started enjoying them I never asked. I had been given a wing in the palace .I was not allowed to enter the main wing where the king lived and in other wings where his sons lived. for four years I lived a very lonely childhood and when I realized that, on a very dark night I left my wing for exploring the palace it was so beautiful and huge then I listen, someone, wailing I tiptoed there .And peaked from the door ,a child was lying on the king size bed adorned in expensive silk cloth. Wailing so hard. There was no one there .So I entered the room and there lay the beautiful baby I have never seen when he saw me he gave me a toothless grin. It felt like he wanted me there he clutched my finger then I heard someone coming so I ran from there to my wing .from that day it became a ritual he cried every night and I went to his room and he grin and clutched my finger sometimes I even slept there on the floor I felt comfort more on that floor then my bed.

It felt like someone is watching over me after some time he stopped crying but I never stopped going to his room .one day I went there and he was waiting for me I came closer and he placed his tiny palm on my face and said" sweet "in his baby voice and grinned. Then I realized I never told him my name. I told him my name was meena. He said no, sweet and his brows drew closer as if he was ready for a fight on this.

"Okay sweet and what is your name "

"Anger"

I knew his brothers' names are like that because their name represented their personalities but he was just a baby how they knew he was anger ,that was not right damn it .

Chapter 4

Meena pov

As he was getting older we started having cute conversations .He told me about his mother who was a good witch.

One day when I was roaming around I heard loud shootings. I followed the noise and heard that someone killed lord general and his wife .They were my parents, they killed my parents.

"No"

Lord said "meena control yourself "

"Lord they killed my parents. I have no one I am an orphan".

" meena, I would take the decision here and you are not an orphan I would do the right thing and you would get the justice I would see to that "

I did not think anyone could provide justice to someone whose parents were killed. Whose dreams were crushed so brutally.The next thing I knew was that lord announced that I was to be the queen of the Lord's fifth state and pledged to Anger.The kid who is only four years old and I was only fourteen. I knew this was a different world it was common for someone to pledge to someone even before they were born but this was too much for me to take in.

How could I rule someone who killed my parents? Was I to be loyal to the murderers of my parents? Think about their good and their happiness and welfare when they took these things away from me and made me a 14-year-old orphan. I was taken to the court and anger was there in the royal guard's arms sleeping blissfully. the poor child did not even know what was happening to him that was even worse to not know that the wrong had happened to you .In Lord's twisted mind it was some kind of punishment to his people to make me their queen and gave me all the powers until his son turned 18.

Chapter 5

Third-person pov.

Meena was standing straight, her back stiffened and anger was sleeping in the guard's arm .the lord in front of the whole court declared them husband and wife till death do them part and queen and king of lord's fifth state.

A fourteen-year-old queen whose parents were killed by her people and now she had to rule them she was all at once an orphan, a weak girl, and a queen with the bravest heart who takes the pledge to always provide for her people and would not think of the past and would be loyal to her husband and her people.

Chapter 6

Meena 14 years old

I entered the court of my state and show them what people did not expect to see firstly my face. they had thought I would not show up. Oh, I would and show them what a woman can do. I would show them I had a backbone .my fears and pain were my own, not theirs to see. I will train myself in every aspect. I would learn to fight like a fierce warrior.

Chapter 7

Third person pov

When queen meena entered the court she did not look like an orphan, or weak, no she looked like a fierce warrior woman ready to fight for her people . she addressed her people and took a vow to protect them against all the forces .she addressed issues no body think she would know.

In the end, the crowd was shouting,"long live queen meena" and she exited the court.

Then I was taken to my chambers. At least they did not expect consummation of the wedding because of my husband's tender age. I enter my room which has a room attached to it. It was the queen and king's bedrooms connected with a door. I opened his room and entered inside. he was sitting on a chair he looked up at me

"Are we husband and wife?"

I looked into his troubled eyes they were so innocent and trusting, I felt protected for him I want to hug him and protect him at least until I could save him from the harsh reality of this cruel dark World where we are all just pawns played by his father, his brothers and our society. I looked into his eyes and put my palm on his shoulder, "honey I am here for you okay it doesn't matter what society says we are but here in this room I am the same lonely girl who you give your friendship and call her sweet, in the coming years they will judge us, demand from us but we have to be strong and believe in each other, whenever you feel like discussing something or feel like you want a friend who never judges, you can come to me and talk about anything without fear of being judged ".

"Why are you talking like big people, can we just play like before "

"Of course, baby we can that's what friends do, they enjoy and we will also enjoy it very much "

"And now you Do not have to come from your wing into mine we can live together like Mumma and papa they are married just as we are now."

"Yes baby now sleep there is a long day ahead of us"

I was in the court when the royal guard came running"queen king anger is breaking all furniture in your rooms he is calling for you and is not listening to anyone, can you please come with me? "

I know why they called him Anger because he had a temper even as a four-year-old kid but it can't be that bad I had always felt sorry for him having that name dictating his personality to everyone even before he developed it for them to see.

"Honey, what are doing?"

"You are my wife you should be here with me "

"Baby listen firstly we are friends and like everyone around us we also have a job to do like my job is to attend the royal court and take the important decisions and yours is to study and prepare yourself for marital arts, you are going to be a king you will have to take important decisions when you will come of age to become the king you do not have that much time and I also need you .you know this is a very difficult job and one always need their friends with them to help them in talking all decision".

"But that's not fair I want to play with you that is why you have given to me, dad said to me you are mine "

"Oh and he did not tell you, you are mine too and now this time I am your guardian I will tell you what to do okay now quit sulking and go to your teacher you will become perfect in everything we will not let our people down, they need us ,our state is not strong like other states, we cannot trust your brothers they had attacked on state earlier they can do that again we cannot be sure even though you are in the state but you have not taken the place on the thrown yet, they can still retaliate because I am on the thrown ",

" They can not kill you, you are my wife "

"We cannot be sure that is why we have to make the state stronger and people confident so they can start trading with other states and do not fear of getting burgled or worst murdered. if we become strong another state's civilians won't attack on us because they know we are powerful and retaliate for our civilian honor.

" you do not worry sweet. I will protect you and our people. I will be your, knight, in shining armor okay?"

"You will be good to your teachers you have to use your anger where it is required at least not on the subject teachers, you can use it when you fight because I know anger gives you strength and makes you feel in control"

"Okay sweet, good day " and he gave a peck on her cheek before going away .

Chapter 8

Third person pov

It looked like magic is on display her every move was so smooth and swift. She sparred like dancing with so much grace. Every soul who saw her knew he can take anyone down. It's been one year since she had come into possession of thrown yet she had proved herself despite being only a girl of 15. her word is law people followed her every rule. because they knew she was the one who will make them powerful. not only she allowed people to trade with outsiders but also provide them with support to do so. She also improved the social living of women. It gave women pride that their ruler was a woman and know what it took to be a woman and be in power in this so-called man's world.

She had also put a royal box in between the capital of the state so that if anyone had any problem they could put it in that box without any fear .they could also keep their name anonymous. Civilians had high hopes for the future with queen Meena ruling their state they could sleep peacefully.

There were rumors also that she was the angel that had given to the lord's son's Anger .no one knew if the tales were true are not but the lord had five sons with dark personalities and because the lord's wife was a good witch and helped eliminate evil from god's world even though she is from the dark world herself. After she fell in love with the lord of our dark world and had her sons God gave her the gift of angels for her sons who would become their light and hope while they would fight the evil that became their personality trait after being sired by the dark lord himself.

It would be entertaining to see whether the lord's kids were better than the lord or not .everyone knew the lord loved his wife and she loved him but they could not live long together because of the Lord's dark personality, the witch lived separately from him but when they could not live apart anymore they started living together then again lord did something devilish that his wife could not handle she started living separately from him.

Chapter 9

Anger 14, Meena 24

I loved Meena but she could be very difficult sometimes. I did everything for her because she is everything to me. I loved her when I was very little and loved her more when we came to live here. she became my wife even though she never considered herself my wife. She said she was only my friend that hurt a lot knowing my wife did not consider herself my wife. still, I was allowed to visit her room whenever I wanted but now she said it could not be allowed any longer because I was a teenager now and it would not be right since I was becoming a man now.

It all happened because of my mistake I should not have started acting on my feeling. I loved her a very long time and loved her a lot but suddenly I started feeling more for her and whenever she laughed with someone or even someone touched her finger I saw the blood I became mad with rage .she was beautiful. my friends visited brothels .it was very common for upper-class men or even if they were boys of 14 to visit brothels and they were served exceptionally well because they are young lads and were mostly gentle with women and they could provide them protection for a longer period and their ego can be easily boosted and sometimes they even fell for them and made them their mistresses.

But I could not do that when I had a beautiful wife at home. who was very intelligent and brave and I felt pride whenever I saw her in court taking difficult decisions with ease. Never had she Shawn distress on her face she was always so calm like she was born to sit there. when I was little I did everything in my training and my studies to make her happy that if I won my sweet Meena would bestow a smile on me and the pride I would see in her eyes for me would be worth my soul and then I started admiring her, wanted to be like her I knew she was good with her sword better than every man better than me and I was the best even though I was14 but I had to be the best because I had to take my place at the age of 18 but I admired her for being better than me. I felt proud but I trained myself more because I wanted to be worthy of her. even worthy of my thrown if I had to be ruler I had to be the best in everything.

So when Meena was bathing in her bathing chamber I entered her room and when I listened to splashing sounds I entered her bathing chamber I could see her back glistening with water droplets, and her hair was in a messy bun. I went forward and kissed her cheek and then the hollow of her neck. I expected anger even somewhere in my fooling heart I expect her to accept my kisses and kissed me back but something I did not expect was for her to laugh at me. she turned and laughed at me, "oh Anger you are a boy just a boy and I am 24 years old women, what do you expect me to kiss you back open my arms and make love to you .you who couldn't even fight better than me, could not control your anger and now it seems you even could not control your lust. You know I could order my man to kill you for entering my room and you boy entered my bathroom without my permission. Go and let those serving girls stroke your ego where you go with your friends."

I knew she had not said anything wrong but it hurt and I never slept with any girl like she said I could not control my anger and grabbed her hair and pulled her toward my muscular chest and kissed her hard and bruised her lips, plunged my tongue in her mouth rubbed her chest against mine and jerked her away "you will control your tongue or I will cut it myself, you will respect me and if I want to take you I can drag you from this tub and can lift your skirt and take you now but no you do not deserve anything, not my love, not even my anger and I knew you did not have any lover in past and if I come to know you are in the market for acquiring one, by God I first kill him then kill you for betraying me ".

Chapter 10

Meena pov

I saw the way he looked at me.His eyes filled with love, adoration, and admiration and by God, it gave me the strength to get going I always considered him a boy .But then I found out that my boy was not a boy anymore he started visiting brothels with his friend, and my outrage knew no bound I was flaming with anger .it did not matter if he was younger than me but still he was my husband and I was always faithful to him and expected the same from him. I knew How every woman saw him .even though he was just 14 years old he was handsome and bravest of all the men and I felt appreciated when he winked at me after winning every fight , every training session .I knew he could easily win with me but he was never concentrated when he fights me .he was always making sure that I did not get hurt . only fights me when I asked him very much.

I knew he had a temper but in his 14 years, it had never been directed towards me until one when I knew that he visited a brothel with his friends and he came into my bathing room when I was bathing. I was already furious with him and his audacity to come into my room after visiting serving girls. He kissed me and I laughed bitterly and blurted out things I could not in my life imagine him saying. I knew I broke his heart and made him a bitter man when he pulled me toward him I could see anger in his eyes and his voice became very hoarse. When he left I sobbed and moaned for two breaking hearts. I never considered in my life that we could live together like husband and wife in this life but I thought at least I could grow older like this being with my friend and when he would marry a woman of his age I could be happy for him. But now I even had no friend and I think today was the day I truly became an orphan. No one would call me his own I wanted to belong to someone but maybe only loneliness was my fate.

Chapter 11

Meena pov

The next day when I woke up I tried to enter his room through my door it was looked from his side in all ten years we lived together they are never looked from either side and then the whole night came crashing down on me so he was that angry with me that he would completely shut me down from his life. When I entered from another entry to his room he was dressed and was going out he saw me but his gaze was impersonal like I was a stranger in a crowd who he would just pass by without even noticing.

" I am sorry Meena I am ashamed of my behavior it would never repeat in the future ever again and I visited the brothel only because my friends dragged me. I was never unfaithful to you and never will be. you will never hear Queen's husband is unfaithful to her, and you will never have to downcast your eyes because of me queen." He was never in my life that formal to me and I do not know whether to feel relief that he was faithful to me." so that's why you locked the room adjoining door from this side

"I do not want to make you feel uncomfortable thinking that I may enter again in your room so to assure you that you do not have to feel unsafe in your own house I locked this and I do not have a key to open this I gave that to your maid "

"Why are you talking like that honey, you know how much I cared for you. you are my only living relation you cannot abandon me too .you are just like others just like my parents who gave me to their lord and then die when I need them and then you who gave me your friendship and then "

"And then what meena, then what?"

"You are leaving me too "

"I am not leaving you meena, how can I leave you my bastard of a father would see to our end himself if we leave each other, marriages do not break that easily in our world that even if it was unwanted like ours "

"Okay then why the hell you are calling me meena or worst queen you never called me meena or queen I am always your sweet, your sweet meena .and what do you just say unwanted our friendship was never unwanted"

"that is your problem you never considered this relationship a marriage always a friendship but never a marriage"

"Because that would be wrong you are a boy and I am a woman always had been older than you and always will be "

"Accepting this as a marriage does not mean we have to consummate it now after I turn 18 then it would be my choice that no one will say you seduced me, hell why would anyone say anything that's our business if I choose to be seduced that would be my decision and what seduction, it will be bound to happen you are my wife, they were the people who got drunk and celebrated the union of our marriage what they said Anger and his angel "

"This marriage will never be consummate ours will always be a relation of friendship that's what I ever wanted and whenever I called you my husband I always felt guilty because you were asleep when your father blessed our marriage but I was awake I could deny in front of everyone "

"Your punishment would be death, how can you deny him, and what was your plan for an heir because this crown will need an heir "

"I thought you could always marry someone else. Divorce cannot be obtained because it was the lord's decision and only the lord can change it"

"You know what meena. I felt sorry for myself that I couldn't understand you that I have always thought at least in this world you would never take my choices away from me, like my father who never discusses anything about my future with me, like my brothers who never thought about me. you are worst than them at least it was expected from them but not from you. I should take your leave queen ".

Chapter 12

Meena pov

For the next four years, Anger was always civil to me but always kept his distance on his 18 birthday he denied the thrown saying that there was unrest in the kingdom as his all brothers are united and they could do anything their father kept them apart as they were ego, sin, mad, grudge and anger if they united they could cause havoc in the world so he did not think it would do any good since they would approach him if they knew he had also become a king and he did not know now what they can do. let her be in power now until they know about his brother's motive whether they wanted to cause havoc in the world or not?

I knew he was telling the truth but I wanted some reaction out of him so I openly disrespect his decision, "you just wanted to be free and live your life as you please if you do not want the responsibility why can't you simply say that? that you are not a man enough to be king to be a responsible man, you just wanted to run from your responsibilities whether it is of becoming a husband or a king, you are a coward man your parents should have named you coward"

"Shut up meena if you do not like my decision we can see to that but you would not disrespect me

I didn't listen to him and just walk out I knew he would be furious but at least he would be something more than a stranger. I entered his room and start shutting the door when he entered and shut it and pinned me to it his chest pressing to mine his arms beside mine caging me he leaned down and kissed me hard " I love you, my husband, I am sorry but I cannot take this anymore I want you you said me it would be your choice. it is your choice honey but I would love it if you choose me "

"I love you my sweet, of course, I choose you, you were always mine you did not know how much I wait for this day when I can choose you and you wouldn't feel guilty for loving and wanting me .say baby, you need me, want me "

"Oh I need you, husband I want you, my love, you pleased me husband I thought you were angry and would never want me "

"I was angry but not anymore I understand you love, my sweet meena you are an honorable woman and I am proud of you "

"You know my brothers contacted me they wanted to ask if I wanted to annul this marriage they would help me as they are united and assure me they did not have any evil intention towards the kingdom they are with their angels and want to meet me and my angel"

"Your angel"

"You my sweet meena you my love truly an angel. I told them I am happy with my life and very happy with my wife and we love to meet them because family should remain united "

"Tell me how they meet their angels"

"My love that's their story to tell and they would tell if anyone wants to listen and we also want to meet readers again with our twin babies "

"First let's make them "
"As you command my queen"